Fluffy Knight
Nighttime Adventures

written by Linh Ly
illustrated by Marco Zerneri

"To my parents and the stuffies in my life."

- Linh

from:
to:

Once it's bedtime,
and you fall asleep,

Fluffy Knight gets up
with a quiet leap.

It's time for Fluffy Knight to do
what he does best,
And that's to make sure you
have a good night's rest.

There are many things Fluffy Knight must do. First, to check for any monsters under the bed that go **boo!**

Blink!
Blink!

Fluffy Knight sees a pair of big, bright lights.

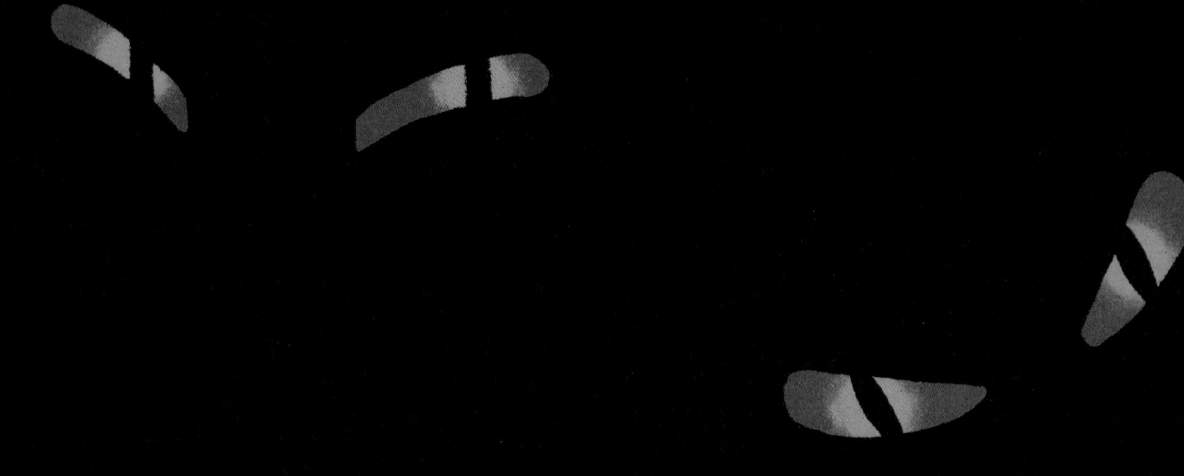

"I will shoo them away," he says since he is a brave knight.

Upon a closer look, he sees they are dust bunnies that fell off the broom.

Fluffy Knight gives them a warning. "Please go now. You can't stay in this room."

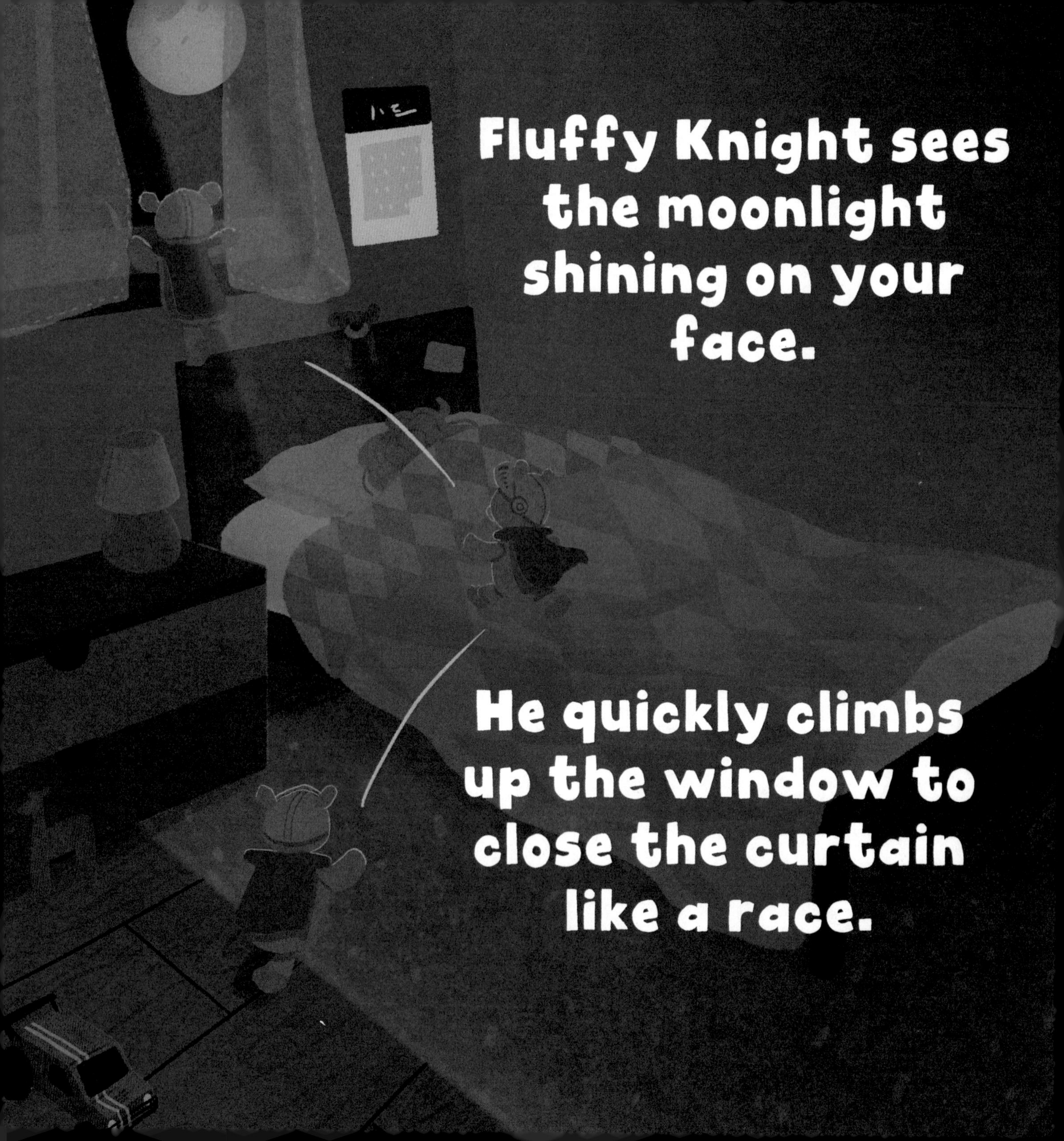

Fluffy Knight sees the moonlight shining on your face.

He quickly climbs up the window to close the curtain like a race.

Fluffy Knight checks on his stuf-
fie friends with a call.
Then all of a sudden... PLOP!
He heard something fall.

"Help! Help!"

cries another bear.
"Oh no! That's my brother Michael who fell down there."

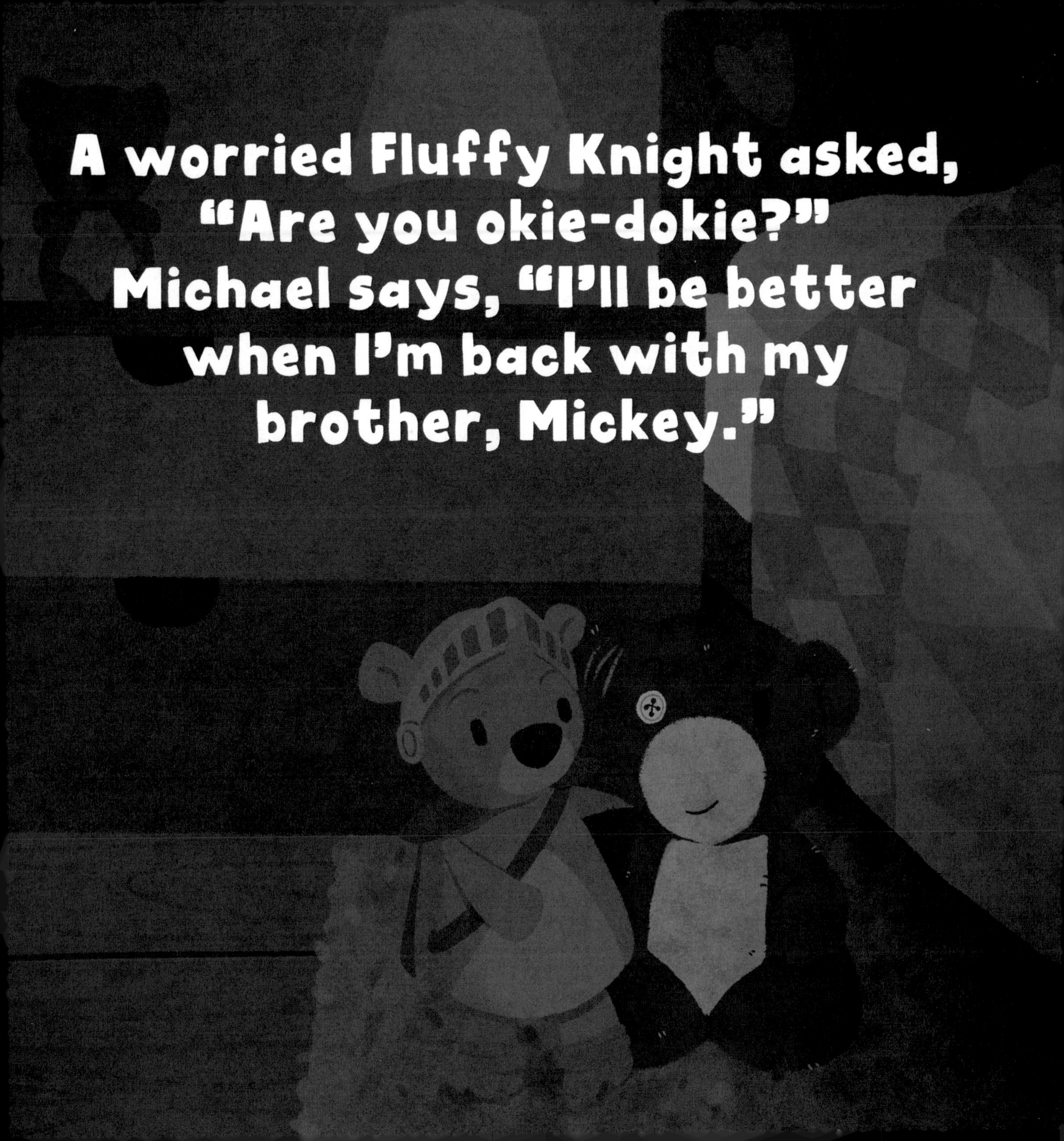

A worried Fluffy Knight asked, "Are you okie-dokie?" Michael says, "I'll be better when I'm back with my brother, Mickey."

Fluffy Knight brings Michael to his brother. They both thank Fluffy Knight, saying,

"You're the best knight
like no other!"

Growl! Fluffy Knight's tummy
just made a big sound.
It's snack time for the knight.
Let's see what he found!

Fluffy Knight is taking a break
with some yummy food.
This puts Fluffy Knight in a
really happy mood.

Fluffy Knight hears noises
on the bed.
"Did you wake up?"
He wondered in his head.

Fluffy Knight checks on you and sees you're having a nightmare.

Being a brave knight, he shoos away the scare.

When the cozy blanket slips
off your shoulder,
Fluffy Knight pulls it back up, so
you won't get any colder.

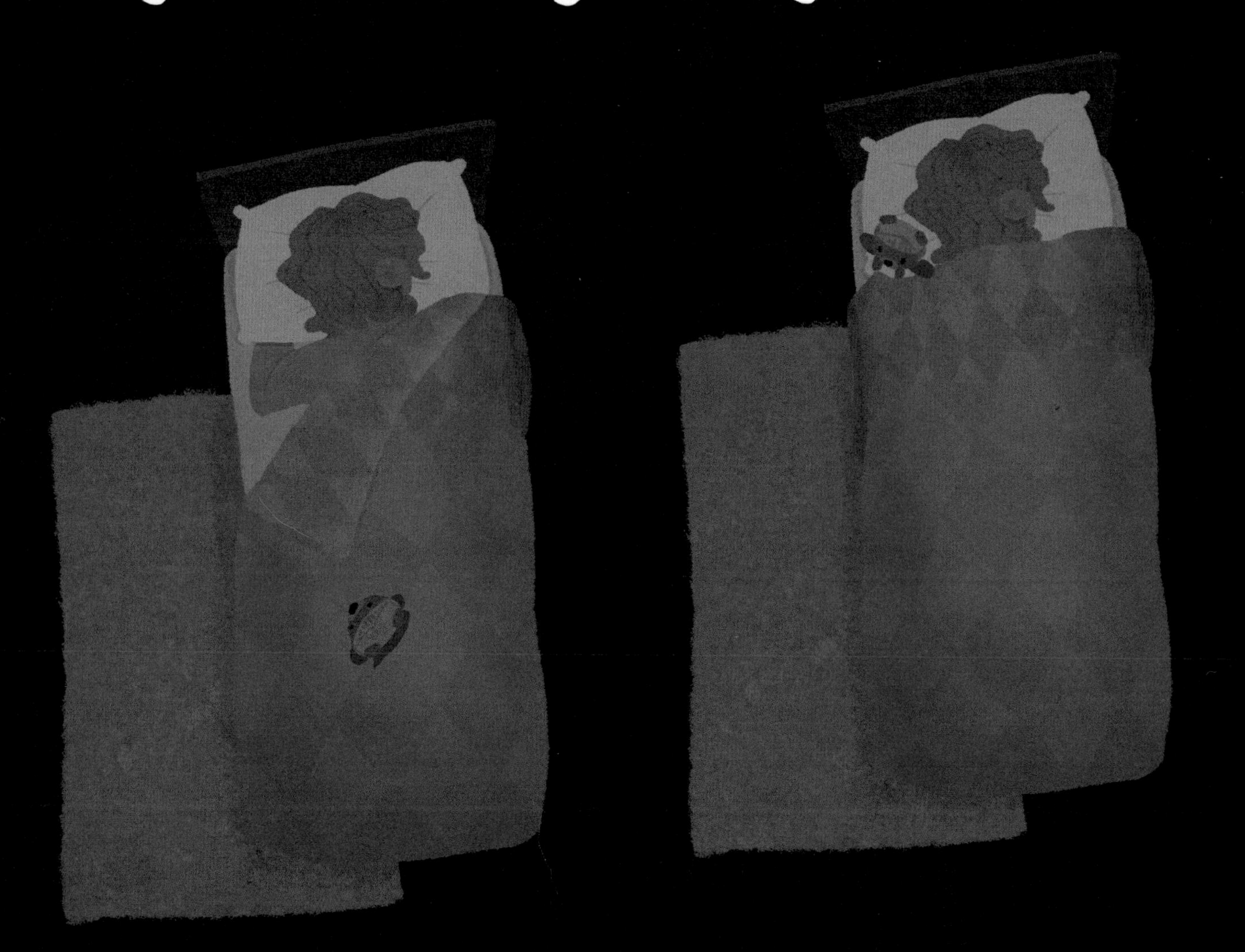

There is a better way to
keep you warm and safe.
That's for Fluffy Knight
to be by your side
right now
and always.

Fluffy Knight: Nighttime Adventures
Written by Linh Ly
Illustrated by Marco Zerneri

ISBN 978-1-7778547-2-0 Hardcover book
ISBN 978-1-7778547-1-3 Electronic book
ISBN 978-1-7778547-0-6 Book

I hope you enjoyed this book! I would love to hear from you.

You can email me at ***linhly.author@gmail.com*** or follow me on

Instagram **@linhly.author**

The Author

Linh Ly is from Toronto, Canada. The Fluffy Knight is her first children's book.

When she was younger, Linh had trouble sleeping, but her fluffy knights came to the rescue.

Mickey and Michael are two of those stuffies that helped her get a good night's rest.

Made in the USA
Columbia, SC
11 October 2021